Having spent her younger years staring up at aeroplanes in the sky, just like Ada and Emily, Zoe has been an airline pilot for 14 years. She is also a very proud mother to her son, Sebastian, whose first home was in St Neots, Cambridgeshire, UK.

ADA AND EMILY
TAKE TO THE SKIES!

ZOE CAMERON

ILLUSTRATED BY NEIL SMITHERS

AUSTIN MACAULEY PUBLISHERS™

LONDON • CAMBRIDGE • NEW YORK • SHARJAH

ISBN 9781398412699 (Paperback)
ISBN 9781398412705 (ePub e-book)

www.austinmacauley.com

First Published (2020)
Austin Macauley Publishers Ltd
25 Canada Square
Canary Wharf
London
E14 5LQ

This book is dedicated to Ada, Brett, Emily, Ethan, Gabriel, Henry, Joshua and my amazing son, Sebastian.

I would like to thank my mum, Karen, for proofreading every single manuscript and for her infinite support. I would also like to thank my dad, Alistair, for being a large part of the inspiration behind the story and my chosen career. Together, my parents have always supported me and made sure I knew that I could be anything I wanted to be in life.

Special thanks to the Virgin Group for allowing me to use their image in an illustration inside this book.

"I've made an important decision!" Ada shouted as she leapt up from where she lay in the centre of the garden. The sudden disruption of the peaceful afternoon caused her dad to jump; the newspaper falling from his face, his afternoon nap seemingly over. He looked up as Ada rushed over, still reclined on his green sun lounger as he retrieved the newspaper from the grass. As Ada raced over, she was half hopping and pulling on her favourite pink trainers, the colour perfectly matching the pink stripes in her blue and pink striped T-shirt which she had paired with dark blue denim shorts.

"I've decided that I want to be a pilot, Dad!" Ada declared.

"I thought that you were going to be an engineer!" he replied. "Well, of course, I'll still be an engineer too! Who else is going to build the aeroplane for us to fly?"

"Us...?" Ada's dad queried.

"Emily is going to be flying with me of course; I'm off to tell her the good news now!"

He smiled as Ada disappeared out of the garden. Placing the newspaper back over his face, he returned to his nap in the afternoon sun.

A few seconds later, Ada was in the garden next door. She immediately spotted Emily lying on the grass, looking up at the sky watching an aeroplane fly high overhead, just as Ada had been doing minutes earlier. Emily was wearing her favourite blue and pink T-shirt, just like Ada. They often turned up in matching clothing, especially when it came to their matching lucky blue and pink striped T-shirts. Having spent the whole of their ten years living next door to each other, they sometimes felt as though each could read the other's mind. Emily had teamed up her T-shirt with bright red shorts and navy-blue flip flops, which were balanced on her toes at the end of her long dark legs. Ada's fair complexion looked pale in comparison to Emily's dark skin which seemed to glow in the summer sun. Emily had pulled her brown coily hair into a ponytail to keep herself cool in the summer heat. Ada had braided her blonde hair into a long plait which hung over her right shoulder.

Emily!" Ada called as she ran over to her best friend. "Ada! I was just going to come and see you! I was watching the aeroplanes flying across the sky and I've made a decision!" Emily said as Ada came and flopped next to her. "I want to be a pilot!" they said in unison. The girls giggled at their joint decision.

"It just looks like so much fun, doesn't it?" said Emily longingly as another aeroplane flew across the sky. "But how are we going to get an aeroplane to fly in?"

Ada grinned at her friend. "Well, you know that go-kart we've been making this summer? I was thinking that with a few adjustments we might be able to turn it into an aeroplane!"

Emily's eyes lit up at her friend's idea. She could see it now! They'd been building a go-kart all summer and had almost finished it, with three weeks left of the school holidays to go. They'd taken it out for a test drive the previous day and it had driven really nicely. There were two seats in tandem, one behind the other. Each seat had a set of pedals and the girls had been amazed at how quickly they had sped through the park. All they had left to do was to paint it—blue and pink of course—and Emily had suggested adding a little cool box in which they could store chocolate. Now, though, the girls were thinking of ways in which to turn their go-kart into their very own aeroplane.

Let's go to your house and use the computer. We need to do some research!" Emily said, already ahead of Ada and running. Her long legs made her easily faster than Ada; within seconds she was kicking off her flip flops and calling 'Hello' to Ada's mum as she ran through the kitchen and into the living room to sit down at the computer. She heard Ada's mum reminding Ada to remove her trainers before Ada appeared next to her at the computer as she searched 'building an aeroplane'.

A few hours later the girls sat back, looked at their notebooks and began comparing ideas. Emily had been making notes on the key points they would need to include to make an aeroplane work. Ada's notebook was full of drawings how to attach the wings and to fit the propellor.

They were about to head down to Ada's shed at the bottom of the garden where the girls had spent much of their summer building their go-kart. It held many other joint inventions from the past few years like the walking robot they had made over the Christmas holidays and the London scene which included a large replica of the London Eye and a working Tower Bridge which they could raise and lower to allow boats to move along on tracks underneath.

Just at that moment Ada's mum popped her head around the door and said, "Emily, your mum has been calling you for the past few minutes, your dinner is about to be served up and Ada, it's time to go and wash your hands for your own dinner, you'll have to carry on with whatever it is you're doing tomorrow."

The girls sighed. They were on a roll, but knew better than to try and argue against dinner time. "See you tomorrow!" Emily said, retrieving her flip flops. Tomorrow was going to be a very big day for them.

Waking early, Ada jumped out of bed and scribbled a few more drawings of ideas that had come to her during the night. She pulled on a pair on purple shorts and a blue T-shirt and raced downstairs. She was about to head straight out to her shed but her mum called after her, "Ada! Wait! Here's your breakfast." She handed Ada two paper bags, knowing Ada wouldn't wait for breakfast, not after the way the two girls had been chatting the previous day! Once they had a plan, there was no stopping them. "Emily's down in your shed already, she got there a couple of minutes ago and I'm guessing that she didn't have time for breakfast either." She smiled as she watched Ada pull on her pink trainers and run out of the back door.

Ada raced into the shed where Emily was at the large white board on the far wall. She grinned as she saw that Emily was wearing her own pair of purple shorts. Emily had drawn a line down the centre of the board and filled the left side with notes. Ada immediately walked over and filled the right side of the board with drawings of her own ideas. They flopped onto the striped beanbags and Ada passed Emily her breakfast. They ate in silence whilst they considered the white board. As soon as they finished eating, they discussed which ideas they liked and started planning. Ada liked Emily's idea to add in a heater to keep them warm as Emily had read that it could get pretty cold up in the air. Emily liked Ada's idea for how to fit the wings to the aeroplane so that they would fold out; this way they could still keep it stored in her shed without having to remove the wings. They jumped up and got to work. Emily started drawing out scale plans and taking accurate measurements whilst Ada got to work taking apart bits of the go-kart that needed adjusting. By lunchtime the girls had made a lot of progress and they ran up to the house just as Ada's dad was about to call them for lunch. As they ran in, Ada handed her dad a piece of paper. What's this?" he asked, taking the note.

"It's a list of the bits we need to be able to complete our aeroplane. Do you think you can help us please?" asked Ada as they tucked into the cheese sandwiches he had made.

"Hmmmm," Ada's dad frowned as he looked down the short list, "give me a moment!" Just as the girls were helping themselves to a second cherry bun, he returned with a pleased smile, rolling his eyes as he noticed the missing buns, "I've just been on the phone to your Uncle Alistair. You know he's been building model aeroplanes for years and he happens to have some wings and a propellor spare from a large-scale model. He said you girls can have them and will pop over in a little while with them."

Ada and Emily grinned at each other. "Thank you!!!" they both cried as they jumped down from the table and raced out and back down to the shed. When Uncle Alistair arrived a couple of hours later, he and Ada's dad knocked on the shed door. Ada opened the door completely covered in splatters of blue paint. Emily appeared beside her with pink paint on her nose and cheek. They saw the wings tucked under Uncle Alistair's arm and the propellor in his hand and threw the door wide open.

Come in!" they both said with huge smiles on their faces. Ada's dad raised his eyebrows at Uncle Alistair. The shed was Ada's domain. It was a rare honour to be invited in. They looked around the shed. There was the whiteboard with the notes and drawings. Along the left side of the shed were the bean bags and on the right side was a work bench covered with tools, pots of paint and various creations by Ada and Emily. In the centre of the shed was their go-kart, now freshly painted in blue and pink stripes. The cool box was in place and there was a small heater next to it waiting to be fitted once they had attached the new wings. Looking back at the girls, Uncle Alistair leant the wings against the work top and gave the propellor to Ada.

"Wow, thank you, Uncle Alistair! These are perfect!" she said, giving him a big hug!

"I've also brought these along for you. Your dad told me you were planning on becoming pilots so I thought they might come in handy," Uncle Alistair said as he gave Ada and Emily a small bag each. They pulled out matching pink leather flying caps, "they've got fleece linings to keep you warm up there, it can get pretty chilly you know."

"Wow!!!" they both squealed, trying on their flying caps, "These are amazing!!!"

"Finally," Uncle Alistair said producing a small brown leather box, which he gave to Ada, "this is a compass. You'll be able to use it so that you know if you're going north to Scotland or south to London."

Ada opened the box and gave her uncle another hug, "This is perfect," she said. Looking at the aeroplane, she knew exactly where she could attach it near the steering wheel so that they would always be able to see in which direction they were heading. Ada's dad and uncle were already being herded towards the door by Ada and Emily. Now they had their final pieces and couldn't wait to finish building their aeroplane.

Several hours later Ada and Emily flopped onto their bean bags, exhausted, covered in paint and beyond excited. They had done it! They'd painted the wings with pink and blue stripes to match the body of the aeroplane. Ada had attached them so that they folded up when in the shed and then folded out straight when they had it outside and ready to fly. The propellor was attached to the front of the aeroplane and driven by the pedals. The heater was fitted to blow warm air onto the girls when it got really chilly.

"It's ready to go!" Emily said happily "shall we take it out for a spin?"

"Great idea!" beamed Ada, pushing herself up to her feet. At that moment the girls heard a loud 'bang' and the shed window filled with light. They had been so busy working that they hadn't noticed the sky becoming dark outside and the thunderstorm moving in. A few seconds later the heavy rain began to fall, hammering against the roof and window of the shed.

"I think we'd better wait," said Emily gazing out at the rain running down the windowpane. "I read it's dangerous to fly in a thunderstorm. It's probably a good idea for us to do some reading on how to actually fly the aeroplane before we set off. Hopefully it will be a nice day again tomorrow."

They raced back to Ada's house and ran into the kitchen soaking wet from the storm.

Ada's mum was in the kitchen and turned around to see the girls dripping water all over the kitchen floor. "Right you two! go and get changed into something dry and I'll throw your clothes into the wash."

"Don't forget my lucky pink and blue striped T-shirt." Ada called as they made their way up the stairs to her room "I'll be needing it ready for our first flight tomorrow!"

Once Ada and Emily were dressed in dry clothes, they returned to find that Ada's mum had been to the library and got some books on flying for them.

"Thank you for these, Mum, they're perfect! Can Emily stay for tea? We want to have a look through them."

"Of course! I've already spoken to Emily's mum; you two looked like you were too involved in your project to send Emily home just yet, not too late though!"

After a dinner of lasagne and salad and another of the cherry buns each Ada and Emily settled down on Ada's bed and started to read. Eventually Ada's mum poked her head around the door and declared it was getting late and it was time for Emily to go home. By now both girls were exhausted. Emily trudged home and Ada pulled the duvet up over herself and fell straight to sleep.

The next day the girls woke up to bright blue skies. They both pulled on their lucky blue and pink striped T-shirts and Ada was just heading out as Emily came running down the path into the garden.

"Come on, slow coach!" Emily laughed as she dashed past Ada and they ran down to the shed. Standing in front of the white board Emily began to make notes. "Ok, so the main things we have to remember are that we have to make sure we have got a really long piece of pavement so that we can get enough speed to take off. After that the main thing to remember is that when we pull the steering wheel towards us we will go up and when we push it away from us we will go down and then we turn the steering wheel side to side to go left and right."

"Great!" grinned Ada. "The park should be quiet now as it's still early and there's that really long straight path so that should be long enough for us to be able to take off. I think we've got everything we need," she said as they wheeled the aeroplane out of the shed.

Oh, don't forget these!" Emily said, darting back into the shed and coming out with their pink flying caps from Uncle Alistair. "Let's go and fly!!!"

The park was deserted as Ada and Emily walked their aeroplane, wings still folded against the sides, up to the far end of the path. As they walked, they checked the condition of the pavement; they wanted to make sure it wasn't going to be too bumpy for when they got really fast. "There's just one bit at the far end," Emily said pointing down the path, "there's a bit of a bump in the pavement that we might have to watch out for if we haven't taken off by then. Right! Let's fix these wings properly in place, shall we?"

Ada set to work folding the wings out and fixing them so that they would stay strong and in place once in the air. A failure of the wings would not be good at all! Once the wings were set, the girls took a step back and admired their creation.

"It looks amazing!" gasped Emily, "I can't wait to take it for a flight! Who's going to take the controls first?"

"You can fly," replied Ada, "you've done most of the reading on how to fly the aeroplane and you were better at driving the go-kart than me. Right, let's give it a go!"

They pushed the aeroplane right to the end of the path to get as much distance as possible and Emily tested the steering wheel to make sure it was connected up correctly to make the aeroplane do what she wanted and checked that the compass was securely fastened in place.

"Ready?" Emily asked pulling on her pink flying cap and looking over her shoulder to the seat behind her where Ada was sat in place with her cap already on her head. Ada nodded with a grin. "Ok, take off, start pedalling!" shouted Emily.

They both began to pedal as fast as their legs could go. They started to move along the path. Faster and faster and faster they went; the propellor spinning ever more rapidly to match their increase in speed. Soon they were nearly at the end of the path.

"Watch the bump!" Ada cried just as they hit it! Bump! They bounced into the air. Ada closed her eyes and winced, expecting them to thump back down on the other side. But they didn't. Opening her eyes again she glanced at Emily who was looking back at her, with the biggest grin Ada had ever seen and realised why. The bump had helped them to take off. They were flying! Up into the air they flew, Emily at the controls, pulling back on the steering wheel to get them higher so that they flew over the top of the trees around the edge of the park.

"Let's test this out properly!" shouted Emily over the noise of the wind, "Are you strapped in properly?" she asked, glancing behind at Ada. Ada checked her seatbelt and gave Emily a thumbs up. "Right, let's give this a go!" Emily said as she rolled the aeroplane to the left gently, starting a circle back around towards the park. Once over the park again, she started to roll to the right again.

"Let's fly over and find our houses!" Ada said excitedly and Emily began another turn back around to the left and they followed the road they had walked along to get to the park. Within a couple of minutes they were over the top of their houses, looking down at Ada's shed.

"This is amazing!" shouted Emily. "We should probably head back to the park and make sure that we can land it though." Ada agreed! They were soon following the road back again to the park. The park was still empty so Emily circled the aeroplane and began to descend as she lined up with the very top of the path from where they had started the take off. She brought the aeroplane lower and lower until finally they bumped back to the ground.

"Use the brakes!" Emily shouted as they raced down the path; Ada sprang into action and applied the brakes they had fitted. The aeroplane was still racing along but getting slower and slower until they eventually came to a stop just before the bump near the end of the path.

The two girls sat in silence for a second, taking it all in before turning to face each other and squealing in excitement. "That was amazing!" they cried. "We actually flew!" grinned Ada "Now we just need to decide where to fly to next! We need a map."

Ada folded the wings back up and they made their way back to Ada's shed. Two paper bags waited just inside the door, each containing a banana, an egg sandwich and a bottle of orange juice; their tummies rumbled in unison as they realised they'd totally forgotten breakfast. Sitting on their beanbags they ate happily whilst discussing where they wanted to fly to first. As they contemplated their first destination, Ada's eyes fell on their model of London.

Emily followed her gaze and they both declared "London!" Now they just needed to work out how to get there. They gulped the last of their orange juice and ran back to the house in search of some maps. An hour later Ada had all of the maps in the house and they were sat on the bean bags in the shed cutting out the pages they thought they would need for the journey from St Neots to London and back. Ada had drawn a map up on the white board including highlighting various landmarks she thought would stand out. She explained to Emily that they could follow the train line all the way to London, pointing out that they should be able to see Alexandra Palace out to the left when they were approaching London and from Alexandra Palace they needed to fly south. When they reached the River Thames, they would find the London Eye.

"Ok, so since I've got the map all sorted in my head, I'll be the navigator and give you directions to get to London. What else do we need?" Ada asked Emily.

"We should probably get some drinks and snacks to take with us," Emily replied, "especially some chocolate! I've got some hidden over at my house, I'll run over and get them. But first..." she said with a growling tummy "it's been a busy day and I'm starving! Let's have some lunch!!!"

Once lunch was complete and the chocolate, snacks and bottles of water were all safely tucked away in the aeroplane, Ada and Emily were just getting ready to take the aeroplane out of the shed when FLASH, BANG!

"Oh no!" Ada groaned "another storm! We'll have to wait until tomorrow morning! We had better make sure we check the weather forecast for tomorrow to make sure it's going to be nice for our flight." Shutting the shed door, they raced up to the house before the rain arrived and spent the afternoon researching the next day's weather and chatting about their first flight and what they would see tomorrow. Ada's mum was surprised to see Emily head off early to go home for her dinner. Ada rushed upstairs after her own dinner to go to bed, calling back to her mum, "I just can't wait for tomorrow to arrive!"

The next morning arrived with beautiful clear blue skies, just as the forecast had promised. There were reports of thunderstorms due later in the afternoon again so the girls knew they needed to get to London and back before the storms arrived. Soon they were wheeling the aeroplane back to the park, dressed in their lucky T-shirts. They had brought so much luck the previous day that they decided they could get another day of wear before their mums would insist on them going through the wash.

They pushed the aeroplane all the way up to the end of the path, and got in, tightened their seatbelts and put on their flying caps. Ada made sure all the maps she needed were secured on a piece of blue ribbon she had found and tied to the aeroplane. It was very important that she didn't lose the maps or they might not be able to find their way back.

After making sure they were ready Emily called, "Take off!" and they both began to pedal as hard as they could, gaining speed rapidly and zooming down the path towards the bump that they knew would help them to get into the air. As they bounced over it Emily pulled back on the steering wheel and they climbed into the air.

"Ok, you need to turn to the left, can you see the rail line?" Ada asked Emily. Emily nodded to confirm she could see the railway line. "Great, you need to turn right now and follow the line."

"I see it," said Emily, "let's pedal harder and climb a bit higher so we can see things more clearly. Once we're high enough we won't need to pedal quite so hard." With a huge effort they climbed a bit higher so they could see the fields around St Neots and the high street and shops. As they started to follow the railway line, they saw a train zoom underneath them on its way to London.

Soon Ada pointed out Alexandra Palace to their left. "Fly over there and then we will turn south. That should take us straight to London," she said as Emily turned the steering wheel. When they were overhead the palace, Ada looked at the compass, "Turn to the right now until I tell you to stop and then you just need to fly in a straight line.........stop!!! Now just fly straight and level and we'll reach the London Eye really soon!"

As they approached London, the girls looked down at the city and gasped with delight. They pointed out the buildings and the parks. They had visited London Zoo in Regent's Park the previous summer and could see it as they headed towards the River Thames.

"There!" said Ada pointing just to the right of the nose of the aeroplane, "there's the London Eye!"

Emily looked in the direction Ada was pointing and saw the giant ferris wheel on the bank of the River Thames. "Stop pedalling," she said to Ada "let's go lower and have a really good look." They both stopped, Emily pushed the steering wheel forwards gently and they began to descend towards the London Eye. It was mid-morning and they could see the wheel rotating. They flew past the ferris wheel and waved back at a group of children who had seen them and were cheering and waving.

"Let's follow the river this way," Ada said, pointing to the west. Emily turned the wheel and then gasped, crying out "Pedal hard! pedal really fast!"

Ada looked up and saw Westminster Bridge right in front of them and the girls pedalled as hard as they could. Emily pulled back hard on the steering wheel and they started to climb. As they approached the bridge, Ada closed her eyes. She heard a loud sigh come from Emily and opened one eye. They had managed to climb enough and were flying over the top of the bridge.

"That was close!" Emily gasped, "but wow! Look, there's Big Ben and the Houses of Parliament!" They followed the river, pointing out parks and buildings as they went. Suddenly they heard a very loud roar above them. Startled, they looked up to see a very large aeroplane passing just over the top of them. Emily shrieked, "Oh my gosh!"

Ada quickly checked the map, "That's London Heathrow airport just there, straight ahead!" she pointed as she turned and looked behind. "There's another aeroplane coming! We have to get out of here! Turn right now and head north!"

Emily did as she was told and turned hard right. "Maybe it's time we go home. My legs are starting to get tired."

Ada agreed, and began to navigate Emily back towards the railway line they had followed into London so that they could follow back it all the way back to St Neots. They climbed up higher again, and once they were as high as they needed to be, Ada leant back and grabbed their water and chocolate from the cool box. "Yummy!" She said as she took a bite of chocolate, "I didn't realise how hungry I am!"

"Mmmm" Emily mumbled as she ate her own chocolate bar and followed the railway line until eventually they reached a curve in the road Ada had marked on the map showing them they were at Biggleswade, so not far to go. Ada guided Emily towards the railway station in St Neots; from there they turned towards the park. To their dismay the girls realised that the park was now full of children playing!

"Oh no! what do we do?" asked Ada as they looked down at their landing path.

"I'm going to take us really low and fly along the path so that everyone knows they need to make way for us," decided Emily.

The girls stopped pedalling and Emily brought the aeroplane down low, rocking the aeroplane from side to side to get everyone's attention as they flew down the length of the path. The children looked up with glee at the sight of the beautiful pink and blue aeroplane flying over them.

"Get off the path!" shouted Ada and they all began to run off onto the grass. Reaching the end of the path they pedalled hard to climb above the height of the trees and Emily looped back around to come in for their final landing.

"All clear!" she said as they descended down to aim at the path. She lined the aeroplane up and landed with a light bump.

"Brakes!" she shouted to Ada, who promptly applied them. They started to slow down until they finally came to a stop, turning to each other as the other children started to run towards them cheering

"Wow!" they said in unison, "That was amazing!"